TIMELESS CLASSICS

THE RED BADGE OF COURAGE

Stephen Crane

– ADAPTED BY –

Emily Hutchinson

SADDLEBACK
EDUCATIONAL PUBLISHING

TIMELESS CLASSICS

Literature Set 1 (1719-1844)

A Christmas Carol
The Count of Monte Cristo
Frankenstein
Gulliver's Travels
The Hunchback of Notre Dame
The Last of the Mohicans

Oliver Twist
Pride and Prejudice
Robinson Crusoe
The Swiss Family Robinson
The Three Musketeers

Literature Set 2 (1845-1884)

The Adventures of Huckleberry Finn
The Adventures of Tom Sawyer
Around the World in 80 Days
Great Expectations
Jane Eyre
The Man in the Iron Mask

Moby Dick
The Prince and the Pauper
The Scarlet Letter
A Tale of Two Cities
20,000 Leagues Under the Sea

Literature Set 3 (1886-1908)

The Call of the Wild
Captains Courageous
Dracula
Dr. Jekyll and Mr. Hyde
The Hound of the Baskervilles
The Jungle Book

Kidnapped
The Red Badge of Courage
The Time Machine
Treasure Island
The War of the Worlds
White Fang

SADDLEBACK
EDUCATIONAL PUBLISHING
www.sdlback.com

ISBN-13: 978-1-61651-091-6
ISBN-10: 1-61651-091-9
eBook: 978-1-60291-825-2

Printed in Guangzhou, China
NOR/0814/CA21401315
18 17 16 15 14   3 4 5 6 7

| Contents |

| 1 |

Fears of Battle

A cloud of fog rose slowly from the cold earth. The rising sun revealed a camp of Union army soldiers stretched out on the hills. Last night the Yankees had seen the red gleam of enemy campfires on a distant hillside. Today, they were hoping for some action.

A tall soldier had gone down to the river to wash a shirt. When he came back he was waving the shirt like a flag.

"I just heard that we're moving out tomorrow, for sure," he said to a group of his comrades. "We're going up the river. Then we'll cut across and catch the Rebels from behind."

"It's a lie! That's all it is—another big lie!" said one private loudly. "I don't believe the darned old army's *ever* going to move.

I've got ready to move eight times in the last two weeks. And we ain't moved yet."

"Believe what you like, Wilson."

The tall soldier, Jim Conklin, was so sure of himself that the men started to believe him. One of them, a young private named Henry Fleming, listened silently while the others talked. Then he went to his tent, crawled inside, and lay on his bunk. He wanted to go over some new thoughts that had come to him lately.

Henry had dreamed of battle glory all his life. The great and bloody wars of his imagination had thrilled him with their sweep and fire. In his daydreams, he had always been a great hero. But Henry was not so sure anymore. Perhaps such battles belonged in the distant past, along with heavy crowns and high castles.

This war seemed different. The soldiers around him seemed more timid. Perhaps religion and education had erased the killer instinct in men.

For months Henry had been burning to enlist in the great war between the North and the South. Tales of great marches, sieges, and conflicts filled the newspaper. He had longed to see it all. But his mother had discouraged him. She gave him hundreds of reasons why he was needed more on the farm than on the field of battle. Then one night the church bell rang to celebrate a great victory over the Confederate army. This news made him shiver with excitement. Later, he had gone down to his mother's room. "Ma," he said, "I'm going to enlist."

"Henry, don't you be a fool!" his mother had replied. Then she had covered her face with the quilt and turned away.

But the next morning he had walked into town and enlisted. When he returned home, his mother was milking a cow. "Ma, I've enlisted," he said to her shyly. There was a short silence. "The Lord's will be done, Henry," she said with a sigh. Then she turned back to the cow.

Weeks later, when he had stepped through the doorway in his new blue uniform, Henry had seen two tears run down his mother's cheeks. As she peeled potatoes, she said,

"You watch out, Henry. Take good care of yourself in this fighting business. Don't go thinking you can lick the whole Rebel army at the start—because you can't! You're just one little fellow among a whole lot of others.

"I've knit you eight pair of socks, and I've put in all your best shirts. I want my boy to be just as warm and comfortable as anybody in the army. When they get holes in them, I want you to send them back to me so I can darn them.

"And always be careful of the company you keep. There's lots of bad men in the army, Henry. The army makes them wild. They like nothing better than to teach a young fellow like you to drink and swear. Keep clear of them, Henry. I don't want you to ever do anything that you would be ashamed to let me know about.

"I don't know what else to tell you, Henry—except that you must never do any shirking on my account. If a time comes when you have to be killed or do a mean thing— why, Henry, don't think of anything except doing what's right.

"Now don't forget about the socks and the shirts, child. I've put a cup of blackberry jam in your bundle. I know you like it above all things. Goodbye, Henry. Watch out, and be a good boy."

He had, of course, been impatient during this speech. It had not been quite what he expected. He was annoyed. When he left the house, he felt a sense of relief.

But Henry looked back when he got to the gate. His mother was kneeling among the potato peels. Her face was stained with tears. She was sobbing. Bowing his head, he suddenly felt ashamed of himself.

On the train to Washington, Henry's spirit had soared. His regiment, the 304th, New York, was cheered all along the way. At every station, there were great spreads of bread and cold meats, pickles and cheese. Henry felt like a hero. Girls smiled at him. Old men patted and complimented him. He felt great strength growing within him.

But after the journey there were months of boring drill in a camp. He had thought that real war was a series of death struggles with little time in between for sleep and meals. But the fact was that his regiment had not done much but sit still and try to keep warm.

Now, as Henry lay in his bunk, a little panic grew in his mind. As he thought about the upcoming battle, he saw terrible possibilities. Springing from his bunk, he began to pace nervously.

Jim Conklin and Wilson came into the tent. They were still arguing. "That's all right," said the tall soldier. "Believe me or not. Pretty soon you'll find out I was right."

Wilson grunted. "Well, you don't know everything in the world, do you?" he said.

"Didn't say I did," Conklin answered.

Henry stopped his pacing. "There's going to be a battle for sure—is that what you heard, Jim?" Henry asked.

"Of course there is," said the tall soldier.

"Thunder!" said the youth.

"Oh, you'll see fighting this time, my boy. Regular out-and-out *fighting*! Why, the cavalry already started to move out this morning."

Henry remained silent for a time. At last he spoke to the tall soldier. "How do you think our regiment will do?"

"Oh, they'll fight all right, I guess, after they once get into it," said the other.

"Think any of the boys will run?"

"Oh, there may be a few. There are some who run off in any regiment. Especially when they first go under fire," said Jim.

"Did you ever think you might run yourself, Jim?" he asked. Henry laughed as if he meant it as a joke.

The tall soldier waved his hand. "Well, if a whole lot of boys started to run, why, I suppose I'd run, too. And if I once started to run, I'd run like the devil. Make no mistake. But if everybody was standing and fighting—why, I'd stand and fight, too. By jiminy, I would. I'll bet on it."

Henry was grateful for Jim's words.

The next morning, the soldiers learned that Jim Conklin's rumor had been wrong. The regiment wasn't going anywhere that day. Some of the men sneered at Jim.

Now Henry had more time to think about his problem. The worst part was that he was afraid to tell anybody how he felt. As the days passed, he grew more afraid that he might run from the coming battle.

By nightfall, the regiment had set up camp in a field. Henry went off by himself and lay down in the grass. The tender blades pressed softly against his cheek.

As he lay there, Henry thought about home. He would have given anything to be making the rounds from the barn to the house. Enlisting had been a mistake. He felt he was not cut out to be a soldier.

Then Henry heard the grass rustling. When he turned his head, he saw the loud soldier coming. He called out, "Oh, Wilson!"

Wilson looked down. "Why, hello there. Is it you, Henry? What are you doing here?"

"Oh, just thinking," said the youth.

Wilson sat down and began to talk about the coming battle. "Oh, we've got 'em now! We'll lick 'em good!" He went on like this, getting more and more excited.

"Oh, you're going to be a real hero, I suppose," said Henry.

"I don't know," said Wilson. "I suppose I'll do as well as the rest."

"How do you know you won't run?"

"Run?" said the loud one. "*Run?* Of course not!" He laughed.

"Well," said Henry, "lots of good men have thought they were going to do great things before the fight. But when the time came, they ran."

"Oh, that's true enough, I suppose," replied the other. "But *I'm* not going to run. The man that bets on my running will lose his money, that's all." The loud soldier nodded confidently.

"Oh, shucks!" said the youth. "I guess you must think you're the bravest man in the world!"

"No, I don't," said Wilson angrily. "I didn't say that. I said I was going to do my share of fighting—that's what I said. And I *am*, too." He glared at the youth for a moment and then got up and walked away.

When Wilson had left, Henry felt absolutely alone. No one else was worried. He seemed to be the only one. Slowly, he went to his tent and stretched out on a blanket. For a long time he stared at the red reflection of a fire on the tent wall. Finally, he fell asleep.

| 2 |

Marching Toward War

The next night the regiment was ordered to move out. The soldiers filed across two pontoon bridges. A glaring fire tinted the waters of the river the color of wine. The insects of the night sang solemnly.

When the regiment got to a camping place, the soldiers slept the brave sleep of wearied men. At dawn they started off again. They kept this up for the next few days. Each night they camped in a different place.

Then one gray dawn, Henry was kicked in the leg by the tall soldier. Before he was quite awake, he found himself running through the woods. But this time was different. Now the men were hurrying, panting, and muttering. His canteen banged upon his leg. His backpack bobbed softly.

His rifle jumped on his shoulder at each step, making his cap bounce on his head. A sudden burst of gunfire came from somewhere in the distance.

The youth could see that the time had come. His manhood was about to be measured. He looked around.

He quickly understood that it would be impossible for him to escape. The regiment enclosed him. He was in a moving box.

As Henry saw this, he realized that he had never wished to come to the war. The newspaper stories had enflamed his mind. He had not enlisted of his free will. He had been dragged by the government. And now they were taking him out to be slaughtered.

Before long, the regiment came upon the body of a dead soldier. The man lay upon his back staring at the sky. He was dressed in an awkward suit of yellowish brown. The youth could see that the soles of his shoes were as thin as writing paper. His dead foot stuck out of one torn shoe. It was as if fate had betrayed the soldier. In death, it showed the man's enemies the poverty which in life he had hidden from his friends.

Henry looked at the dead soldier's gray face. The wind raised the man's blond beard. It moved as if a hand were stroking it. The regiment slowed down to look but kept on marching.

Now a great wave of fear swept over Henry. Suddenly *everything* seemed wrong. It occurred to him that the generals did not know what they were doing. It was all a trap. Henry and his comrades were all going to be sacrificed. The generals were stupid. The enemy would soon swallow them all.

Henry thought that he should warn the others. Why should they be killed like pigs? The generals were idiots to send them marching into a death trap! But Henry could not speak. He saw that even if the men were afraid, they would laugh at his warning. They would jeer him.

After a time, the brigade stopped in a forest. They began to build a low wall of stones, sticks, earth, and anything else they could find. The air was hazy with gunsmoke. In a short time, there was quite a barricade along the front. Soon, however, the men were ordered to move once more.

The men went up a hillside and continued along the top of the ridge. From there, Henry could see men running. He could also see flashes of fire from the rifles. Clouds of smoke were drifting across the fields like ghosts. The terrible noise was like the roar of an oncoming train.

As Henry crouched down to watch, he felt a heavy hand upon his shoulder. Turning, he saw Wilson, the loud soldier.

"It's my first and last battle, old boy," said Wilson. He was deathly pale and his lips were trembling. "Something tells me—"

"What?"

"I'm a dead duck this first time and . . . I want you to take these things to my folks." He ended in a sob of pity for himself. Then he handed Henry a little packet done up in a yellow envelope.

"Why, what the devil—?" said the youth.

Wilson gave him a look as from the tomb. Saying nothing more, he raised a limp hand in farewell and turned away.

The regiment marched down from the ridge and stopped near a grove. As the men were getting into position, a shell came screaming in just above their heads. Exploding in the trees, it showered them with damp brown earth and pine needles.

Then bullets began to whistle among the branches. Twigs and leaves came sailing down. Henry and the others dodged and ducked their heads to avoid getting hit.

But the lieutenant had been shot in the hand. He began to swear so loudly that a nervous laugh passed down the regiment line. It was as if the man had hit his fingers with a hammer at home. The captain of the company ran up. With his sword tucked under his arm, the captain began to bind up the lieutenant's wound with his own handkerchief. The two of them argued about how the binding should be done.

Suddenly, wild yells came from behind the walls of smoke. A mob of Union soldiers came running toward them. Two officers on horseback galloped about, screaming orders. But the fleeing men paid no attention to the officers' commands. They swept past Henry's regiment and kept on running.

The men in Henry's regiment were breathless with shock. "My God! Saunders has gotten crushed!" whispered a corporal at Henry's elbow. Henry hadn't seen whatever it was that caused these men to run. But he resolved to get a view of it. And then, he thought, he might very likely run faster than any of them.

| 3 |

The Test

"Here they come!" a voice called out.

There was rustling and muttering among the men. For protection, they tried to pull some empty ammunition boxes around them into various positions.

Then the cry was repeated. "Here they come! Here they come!" Gun locks clicked. Across the smoke-filled fields came a swarm of running men. A Rebel flag, tilted forward, sped near the front.

In his excitement, Henry was startled by the thought that maybe his gun was not loaded. He tried to remember the moment when he had loaded it, but he could not.

The colonel began scolding his men. The man at Henry's elbow started shaking and mumbling to himself, "Oh, we're in for it now!

Oh, we're in for it now!"

Perspiration streamed down Henry's face. He wiped his eyes with his coat sleeve. He stared at the enemy soldiers crossing the field in front of him. Somehow he instantly stopped worrying about whether his rifle was loaded. He fired a first wild shot.

At that moment Henry stopped thinking about himself. He became not a man but a member. And that something of which he was a part was in danger. Now he could not run—no more than a little finger can run from a hand.

Suddenly Henry became sharply aware of his comrades about him. He felt a strong sense of brotherhood with all of them. This feeling was much stronger than his feeling for the Union cause.

Henry was at a task—like a carpenter working as hard as he could at his job. Soon he began to feel the effects of the fighting. First there was a blistering sweat. His eyeballs felt like hot stones about to crack. A burning roar filled his ears.

Then Henry began to feel a red rage.

Suddenly he hated his rifle, which could only be used against one life at a time. He hated the smoke, the noise, and the heat. He wished that he could wipe out the enemy with a single blow.

Many of the men were calling out, muttering, and groaning. The man at the youth's elbow was babbling like a baby. The tall soldier was swearing in a loud voice. There were cheers, snarls, and prayers. The officers rushed around roaring commands.

The man right next to Henry had been grazed by a shot. Blood streamed down his face. He clapped both hands to his head and ran. Farther up the line, a man had his knee splintered by a ball. Immediately he had dropped his rifle and gripped a tree with both hands. And there he still remained, clinging and crying for help.

At last an excited yell went along the line. The firing died down to a few stray pops. As the smoke slowly drifted away, the youth saw that the charge had been beaten back. The enemy had retreated!

Up and down the line, men were talking.

"Well, we've held 'em back. Darned if we haven't!" The men smiled at each other.

Henry turned to look behind him and off to the right and left. He saw motionless forms on the ground. Arms were bent. Heads were turned in incredible ways. It seemed that the dead men must have fallen from the sky to get into such positions.

As he gazed around, Henry noticed the pure blue sky and the sun shining on the trees and fields. It was surprising that Nature had calmly gone on with her business in the middle of such horror.

So it was all over at last! The supreme test had been passed. Then suddenly, cries of warning again broke out. "Here they come! They're coming back!"

The youth turned quick eyes upon the field. Again he saw the tilted Rebel flag speeding forward. Again, shells came swirling through the air, exploding in the grass or among the leaves of the trees. To Henry, they looked like strange war flowers bursting into bloom.

The men groaned to one another. "Oh, say, this is *too much* of a good thing! Why can't the generals send us some support? I didn't come here to fight the whole darned Rebel army."

The youth stared. Surely, he thought, this impossible thing was not about to happen. He waited as if he expected the enemy to suddenly stop, apologize, and leave with a bow. Surely it was all a mistake.

But the firing began somewhere in the middle of the regiment and ripped along quickly in both directions. As the exhausted men swung into action, Henry lifted his rifle and joined them.

Peering through the smoke, he saw that the field was covered with running and yelling men. A man near him, who up to this time had been working hard with his rifle, suddenly stopped. Then he turned and ran away howling. Soon another man also fled. Henry saw that there was no shame in his face. He ran like a rabbit.

Henry watched the fleeting forms of more men scampering away. He yelled with fright. Then he, too, began to speed toward the rear in great leaps. His rifle and cap were gone. His unbuttoned coat flapped in the wind. His canteen, on its thin cord, swung out behind.

Henry ran like a blind man. Two or three times he fell down. The noises of the battle seemed like stones about to crush him. Mingling with others as he ran, he heard footsteps pounding behind him. It seemed that the whole regiment was fleeing.

The sound of so many footsteps gave him his one hope. Surely death must make a first choice of the men who were nearest. That's why there was a race.

As the youth plunged ahead, he lost his sense of direction. Finally he came to a small clearing in the woods. He could see a general on horseback surrounded by other mounted officers. They were all listening closely to a colonel who had just ridden up to give them news of the battle.

After a moment, the general bounced excitedly in his saddle. "Yes, by heaven, they've held 'em!" His face beaming upon the earth like a sun, the general kept repeating, "They've *held 'em*, by heaven!"

| 4 |

Fallen Soldiers

Henry realized that the general was talking about his regiment. By heaven, they had won after all! He could hear cheering. Now Henry felt amazed—and angry, too.

He had fled for good reasons. Wasn't it the duty of every little piece to save itself if possible? Later, the officers could fit the little pieces together again, and make a battle front. If none of the little pieces were wise enough to save themselves, how could the army fight another day? It was clear that he was right.

Thoughts of his comrades came to him. The blue line had withstood the enemy's blows and won. This made him feel bitter and angry at his comrades. He knew it could be proved that they had been fools.

He wondered what they would say when he

appeared in camp later. In his mind he could already hear their howls and jeers.

The longer he thought about it, the more he began to pity himself. His eyes took on the look of a criminal who thinks his guilt is but little and his punishment too great.

Slowly he moved from the fields into a thick woods, as if he wanted to bury himself.

After a time, the sounds of rifle fire grew faint, and the cannon boomed in the distance. The sun blazed among the trees. A woodpecker stuck its head around the side of a tree. A bird flew by on light wings.

Henry threw a pine cone at a squirrel, and the little creature ran with chattering fear. The youth felt triumphant at this. That was the law of Nature, he thought. The squirrel, seeing danger, had run away without ado. It did not stand up to the missile and die with an upward glance at the heavens. No. It had fled as fast as its legs could carry it. The youth felt that he and Nature were in agreement. She backed up his arguments.

Reaching a clearing in the woods, Henry stopped, horror-stricken at what he saw.

Henry was being stared at by a dead man seated against a tree. The corpse wore a uniform that had once been blue. The eyes had changed to the dull color of a dead fish. The mouth was open. A crowd of ants ran over the gray skin of the face.

The youth gave a shriek. The dead man and the living man exchanged a long look. Then Henry turned and fled through the underbrush. In his mind he could still see the black ants swarming upon the gray face, moving horribly toward the eyes.

After a time Henry stopped running. The sun sank until slanted bronze rays struck the forest. Henry's mind flew in all directions as he tried to sort out his feelings. Hearing the sounds of battle in the distance, he began to run in the direction of the fighting. He saw that it was ironic that he was running *toward* that which he had run *from*.

Soon he could see long gray walls of smoke. Thundering booms of a cannon shook him. The loud crack of rifle shots hurt his ears. For a moment he gawked in the direction of the fight. Then he went on again. The battle fascinated him. He felt he must get close to it.

He came to a fence and climbed over. On the far side, the ground was littered with clothes and guns. A folded newspaper lay in the dirt. A dead soldier was stretched out with his face hidden in his arm. Farther off Henry could see a group of five corpses keeping sad company. A hot sun blazed down upon the spot.

Henry felt like an invader. Surely this forgotten part of the battleground was owned by the dead men. He felt that one of them might rise and tell him to be gone.

Finally Henry came to a road. A blood-stained crowd of wounded soldiers went streaming by. They were cursing, groaning, and wailing. One had a shoeful of blood. He hopped like a schoolboy in a game, laughing strangely. Another man was swearing at the general and blaming him for his wounds.

Henry joined this crowd and marched along with it. A tattered man limped along quietly at Henry's side. He was covered with dust, blood, and powder stains from his hair to his shoes. In a shy way, he tried to offer Henry his friendship. The youth quickly noticed that the soldier had two wounds. The one on his head was bound with a blood-soaked rag. The other wound made his arm dangle like a broken tree branch. "It was a pretty good fight, wasn't it?" the tattered soldier asked.

"Yes," said Henry. He walked faster to get away, but the soldier kept up with him.

"Don't you think it was a pretty good fight?" he said again. "Darned if I ever saw fellows fight so well. I *knew* it would turn out this way. You can't lick these tough Yankee boys. No, sir! They're *fighters*! Not one of our boys ran away once the fighting started."

He glanced at Henry, but the youth looked straight ahead and said nothing. Then the tattered man asked in a brotherly tone, "Where were you hit, boy?"

The youth felt instant panic at this question. "Why," said Henry, "I—I—that is—" Then suddenly he turned away and slid through the crowd. The tattered man looked after him in amazement.

| 5 |

Red Badges

Once the tattered man was out of sight, Henry fell back into the procession.

But the man's question had made him nervous. Now he felt that his guilt and shame could be seen by all.

He looked at the grimy, wounded soldiers with envy. He wished that he, too, had a wound—a red badge of courage.

In the crowd ahead, Henry noticed a tall man walking along stiffly. The man seemed to be looking for a special place, like someone choosing a grave. As Henry got closer, he jumped as if bitten. Rushing forward, he laid a hand upon a tall man's arm. As the man turned, Henry screamed, "Gawd! *Jim Conklin!*"

Jim smiled and said, "Hello, Henry."

The youth stuttered and stammered. "Oh, Jim—oh, Jim—oh, Jim—"

The tall soldier held out a bloody hand. "Where have you been, Henry?" he asked. "I thought maybe you got killed. You know, I was out there." He pointed in the distance. "And, Lord, what a circus! I got shot. Yes, I got shot." He repeated this as if he did not know how it came about.

The two friends marched on. Suddenly, the tall soldier seemed to be overcome with terror. His face turned gray. He began to speak in a shaky whisper. "I'll tell you what I'm afraid of, Henry," he said. "I'm afraid I'll fall down. And then one of those darned artillery wagons will run over me. That's what I'm afraid of." His eyes rolled in wild terror.

The youth cried out, "I'll take care of you, Jim! I swear to God I will!"

Then the tall soldier seemed to forget all his fears. Now he brushed Henry aside, saying, "No—no—leave me be—leave me be—" Stumbling, he lurched ahead, and Henry had to follow.

Soon Henry heard a voice talking over his shoulder. Turning, he saw that it was the tattered soldier. "You'd better take him off the road, partner. There's a battery coming fast down the road. He'll get run over. He'll be gone in five minutes anyhow. You can see that. Where in blazes does he get his strength?"

"Lord knows!" cried the youth.

Henry ran forward. "Jim! Jim!" he said. "Come with me."

Jim turned to face Henry. "Leave me be,

can't you?" He let out a deep gasp.

Then the tall soldier started to run ahead. Henry and the tattered soldier followed him. They saw him stop suddenly and stand still. He looked as if he had at last found the place he had been looking for. Then his chest began to heave. His eyes rolled, and his legs began to shake. Finally his body seemed to stiffen. Slowly, he swung forward like a falling tree. His left shoulder struck the ground first.

Henry rushed over to his friend and gazed upon his gaunt face. His mouth was open and the teeth showed in a laugh. His bloody jacket had fallen away from his body. The man's side looked as if it had been chewed by wolves.

With sudden rage, the youth turned toward the battlefield. He shook his fist. "Hell—" he cried. The red sun was pasted in the sky like a wafer.

The tattered man looked at the corpse. "Well, he's gone now, isn't he?" he said. "We might as well begin to look out for ourselves. And I must say I'm not enjoying any great health myself."

Henry saw that the tattered man's face was turning blue. "Good Lord!" he cried. "You're not going to—not you, too!"

The tattered man waved his hand. "Not me. Well, there's no use in our staying here. Your friend can't tell us anything now.

"And you don't look so good either. I bet you've got a worse wound than you think. You better take care of it. It doesn't do to let such things go. Now where is it you were hit?"

The youth made an angry motion with his hand. "Oh, don't bother me!" he said.

"Well, Lord knows I don't want to bother anybody," said the man.

Henry had been struggling with his feelings. Now he looked with hatred at the tattered man. "Goodbye," he said coldly.

The man looked at him in amazement. "Why, partner—where are you going?"

"Over there," said Henry, pointing.

"Well, now look here—this won't do," said the tattered man. "It's not right for you to go off with a bad hurt—it's not *right*!"

Henry climbed a fence and started away.

Turning at a distance, he saw the tattered man wandering helplessly about in the field.

The simple questions of the tattered man had been like knife thrusts to Henry. They made him feel that he could not keep his crime hidden. Sooner or later it was sure to come out in the open. Everyone would know he was a coward.

| 6 |

Henry Gets Hurt

The roar of the battle was growing louder. Great brown clouds of smoke made it hard to see. Then, coming around a small hill, Henry saw the road again.

A column of soldiers was marching swiftly toward the battle. Something about them showed a fine feeling that nothing mattered so long as they got to the front in time. As the youth watched, a black cloud fell over him. He could *never* be like them. He felt like crying.

To Henry, their haste to reach the battle seemed even more noble than the actual fighting. They were heroes. Men like that could sleep with perfect self-respect. If only he could exchange lives with one of them!

Then his problems began to drag at him.

He had no rifle. He could not fight with his hands, he said to himself. Well, rifles could be found. Also, he thought, how could he ever find his regiment? Well, he could fight with *any* regiment.

The more Henry thought, the worse he felt. He could not join these men. He wasn't at all like them. He could never be a hero.

Yet, like a moth drawn to a flame, he was drawn on toward the battle. He had a great desire to see, and to get news. He yearned to know who was winning.

Henry told himself that he had never lost the desire for a victory. Yet, he knew that a defeat for the army might be good for him. In a defeat, *many* brave men might desert the colors and run like chickens. Then he would appear as one of them. It would be easy to believe he had not run any farther or faster than they. And if he himself could believe this, others might believe it, too.

In a defeat, he wouldn't look so bad. It might even seem that he fled early because he had better judgment than the others.

Henry tried to push these thoughts away.

He thought he must be the most selfish man in the world. In a way, he envied the corpses. They might have been killed by lucky chances, before they could run. Yet they would be honored by history.

Now he started to think of an excuse. What fine tale could he take back to his regiment?

He thought of many stories, but threw them aside one by one. Even he was quick to see holes in them all. He could imagine everyone was saying, "Where's Henry Fleming? He ran, didn't he?" They would question him with sneers, and laugh at him.

Then suddenly Henry saw a dark wave of men come sweeping out of the woods. Wild-eyed, they charged toward him like terrified buffaloes.

The youth was horror-stricken. Frozen, he stared at them in amazement. Was the fight lost? Within him something cried out, "Why—what—what's the matter?"

Soon they were leaping and scampering all about him. Their frightened faces shone in the dark. The youth turned from one to another of them as they ran by him. His questions were lost. No one seemed to see him.

Finally Henry clutched a man by the arm. For a moment they swung around face to face. "Why? *Why?*" stammered the youth.

"Let go of me! Let *go* of me!" screamed the panting, red-faced man. Because Henry would not let go, the man slammed his rifle down on Henry's head, and then ran on.

A blinding light flashed before Henry's eyes, and something like a roar of thunder exploded inside his head. His legs seemed to die, and he sank to the ground. Trying to rise, he was like a man wrestling with a creature of the air. It was a terrible struggle. Every time he tried to get up, he fell back weakly.

At last, with a twisting movement, he got up on his hands and knees. Then, like a babe trying to walk, he got to his feet. Pressing his hands to his head, he staggered forward.

Henry touched the wound. The pain of the contact made him draw a long breath. His fingers were covered with blood.

The blue haze of evening was now upon the field. Henry went lurching on as the dusk deepened. He could barely see where he was going.

Soon his wound pained him very little. But he was afraid to move fast, for fear of disturbing it. Holding his head very still, he tried not to stumble. He imagined blood dripping under his hair.

Henry grew weary. His shoulders were stooped as if he were carrying a great bundle. Like an old man's, his feet shuffled along the ground. He wondered whether he should stop and sleep.

Just then he heard a cheerful voice say, "You seem to be in a pretty bad way, boy."

The youth did not look up.

The owner of the cheery voice took him firmly by the arm. "Well," he said with a laugh, "I'm going your way. The whole gang is going your way. Let me help you." So they began to walk along together, like a drunken man and his friend.

As they moved through the forest, the man questioned the youth. "What regiment do you belong to? Eh? What's that? The 304th New York? Oh, they're way over in the center—a long way from here. How did you get so far away, anyhow? I wish we were sure of finding our regiments tonight. But I guess we can do it."

The man seemed to have an amazing sense of direction. He kept talking as he led the youth through the tangled forest. Now and then they met up with soldiers on guard duty. The man seemed to know just what to say.

At last, the man began to chuckle with glee. "Ah, there you are! See that fire? See those wagons? Well, that's where your regiment is. And now, goodbye, old boy. Good luck!"

Shaking Henry's hand, he walked off into the night, whistling cheerfully. As the man disappeared into the night, Henry realized that he had not once seen his face.

| 7 |

Back with the Regiment

Henry walked slowly toward the campfire. Suddenly a voice called out, "Halt! Halt!" The sentry's voice sounded familiar. Henry called out, "Hello—Wilson, is that you?"

The loud soldier came slowly forward. "I can't believe it. That you, Henry?"

"Yes, it's—it's me."

"Well, well, old boy. I'm glad to see you! I thought you were dead, sure enough."

Henry could barely stand on his feet. But he wanted to tell his story now—before anyone could learn the truth. He began, "Yes, yes. I've—I've had an awful time. I've been way over on the right—separated from the regiment. I got shot. In the head."

His friend stepped forward quickly. "What? Got *shot*? Why didn't you say so?"

Another man came up to them. They could see that it was the corporal. "Why, hello, Henry—you here? I thought you were dead. Where were you?"

"Over on the right. I got separated."

"Yes, and he got shot in the head, too. We've got to take care of him," said Wilson.

Wilson and the corporal led Henry over to the fire. Then Wilson went back on guard duty. "Now, Henry," said the corporal. "Let's have a look at your old head."

The youth sat down. The corporal began to

examine Henry's head. "Ah, here we are!" he said. "Just as I thought. You've been grazed by a ball. Looks like it stopped bleeding a long time ago."

The corporal got up. "By morning your head will feel hot and dry. And you may feel sick. But you'll be OK. Now, you just sit here and don't move. I'll send Wilson back here to take care of you." The corporal left.

Henry stared into the fire with a vacant look. After a while, Wilson came along, carrying two canteens. He gave Henry a canteen full of coffee. "Well, now, Henry, old boy," said Wilson. "We'll have you fixed up in a minute." As Henry drank the coffee, Wilson took out a handkerchief. He folded it like a bandage and poured water from the other canteen on it. Then he bound the handkerchief over Henry's head. He tied the ends in a knot at the back of Henry's neck.

"There," he said. "Now come on. Let's see that you get a good night's rest." He helped Henry to his feet. Then he led him carefully through all the sleeping soldiers who were lying on the ground. Soon he stooped and picked up his own blankets. He spread the rubber blanket on the ground and placed the woolen one about Henry's shoulders. "There now," he said. "Lie down and get some sleep."

The youth got down and stretched out. The ground felt like a soft couch. Suddenly he said, "Hold on a minute! What are *you* going to sleep in? I've got your—"

The loud young soldier said, "Shut up and go to sleep. Don't act like a fool."

Henry said no more. An exquisite drowsiness had spread through him. Hearing a splatter of gunfire from the distance, he gave a long sigh and fell deeply asleep.

When he awoke, Wilson came over. His arms were filled with kindling for the fire. "Well, Henry, how are you feeling this morning?" he asked.

The youth yawned again. His head felt as big as a melon. "Oh, Lord, I feel pretty bad."

"Shucks! I'd hoped you'd feel better this morning. Come now, and get some grub. Maybe that will fix you up."

At the fireside, Wilson watched over Henry

with tenderness and care. He poured coffee and roasted some fresh meat. Finally he sat down and watched Henry eat.

The youth noticed an amazing change in his friend from just the other day. No longer was Wilson so loud and boastful. He didn't seem to have a need to swagger and brag anymore.

Wilson balanced his coffee cup on his knee. "Well, Henry," he said, "do you think we'll wallop 'em?"

The youth thought for a moment. "Day before yesterday, you would have bet *you'd* lick the whole Rebel army by yourself."

His friend looked amazed. "Would I?" He thought a minute. "Well, perhaps I would." He stared humbly at the fire. "I guess I was a pretty big fool in those days." He spoke as if years had passed. "Anyway, the officers say that now we've got the Rebs just where we want 'em."

"I don't know about that," Henry said. "It looked as if we were getting a good pounding yesterday." Then a sudden thought came to him. "Oh! Jim Conklin's dead."

"*What?* Is he? Jim Conklin?"

"Yes. He's dead. Shot in the side."

"You don't say so. Jim Conklin . . . poor guy." There was a long pause. Then Wilson went on, "You know, the regiment lost over half its men yesterday. I thought they were *all* dead—but they kept coming back last night. So it turns out that we only lost a few. They'd been scattered all over. Some of the men were fighting with other regiments—just like you."

"So?" said the youth.

| 8 |

Another Battle

The men were waiting for the command to march. Suddenly the youth remembered the little packet that Wilson had given him. "Wilson!" he called out.

"What?" answered Wilson, moving to Henry's side.

Then the youth suddenly decided not to bring up the subject. "Oh, nothing," he said. It was still in his pocket, the bundle of letters wrapped in a faded yellow envelope.

Henry had seen how easily he could be hurt by Wilson's questioning. The packet would be a small weapon to use at the first sign of a cross-examination. In a weak hour, Wilson had spoken with sobs of his own death. But he had not died. Thus, he had delivered himself into the hands of the youth.

Henry felt superior to his friend. His own pride was now entirely restored. No one would find out he had run. After all, his own mistakes lay hidden in the dark, so he was still a man. A little flower of confidence began to grow within him.

He remembered how some of the men had run from the battle. As he recalled their terror-struck faces, he felt scornful. They were weak. As for himself, he had fled with dignity. Suddenly Wilson's voice broke into Henry's thoughts. "Fleming!" he said.

"What?" said Henry.

"Well, I guess you might as well give me back those letters," Wilson gulped.

"All right, Wilson," said the youth. He loosened two buttons of his coat. Thrusting in his hand, he slowly brought forth the packet. As he held it out to his friend, Wilson turned his face away.

Henry saw that Wilson was suffering an attack of shame. As Henry studied him, he felt pity for his friend. "The poor devil, it makes him feel bad!" he thought.

Before too long, the regiment was ordered

to move again. As they retreated through the woods, they could see the enemy coming after them. At this sight, Henry exploded in anger. "By God, our general is a lunkhead!" he shouted.

Wilson said, "Oh, well, what if we got licked this time? Maybe it's not the general's fault—not altogether. He did the best he could. It's just our bad luck."

"Well, don't we fight like the devil? Don't we do all that any men could?" demanded the youth loudly. He was secretly surprised that he had spoken these words. He looked about him, but no one questioned his right to say such things. "Didn't we do better than most other regiments?"

Wilson's voice was stern. "No man will ever dare say we don't fight like the devil. But still, we don't seem to have any luck."

"Well, then, if we fight like the devil and don't ever win, it *must* be the general's fault," said Henry. "And I don't see any sense in fighting and fighting if we're always going to lose. And all because of some darned old lunkhead of a general."

The troops were at last halted in a clearing. Soon the regiment formed a line facing the enemy infantry. Now the sun was directly overhead. As its rays reached down into the gloomy woods, the noise of gunfire broke out. Suddenly, the woods began to crackle as if afire.

"Good God," the youth grumbled. "We're always being chased around like rats! It makes me sick. Nobody seems to know where we go or why we go."

Wilson cut in with a calm voice. "It'll turn out all right in the end," he said.

"Oh, the devil it will!" said Henry. "Don't tell me. I know—"

"You boys shut right up," cried the lieutenant. "All you've got to do is fight."

Just then, a single rifle flashed from a thicket in front of the regiment. In an instant it was joined by many others until the battle roar settled to a rolling thunder.

The men of the regiment were exhausted. They rolled their eyes toward the advancing battle. Some shrank and flinched. As if in a trance, they stood like men tied to stakes.

| 9 |

Henry as Hero

Henry began to fume with rage. How dare the enemy give him no rest, no time to sit down and think! Those Rebels seemed never to grow weary. Well, he would not be treated like a kitten chased by boys. Men driven into deadly corners might develop teeth and claws.

The youth's eyes burned with hate, and his teeth set in a snarl. The winds of battle swept all through the regiment. Henry did not know that he was standing on his feet and firing his rifle. He lost awareness of everything but his hate. The flames bit into him. The barrel grew so hot that his hands were burning. But he kept on stuffing cartridges into it and pounding them with his clanking, bending ramrod.

At last the enemy seemed to be falling

back. Seeing this, the youth instantly charged forward, like a dog chasing a retreating foe. Then he realized that he was still firing when those around him had stopped. He was so engrossed that he was not aware of a lull.

Someone cried out, "You fool! Don't you know enough to quit when there isn't anything to shoot at? Good God!"

He turned and looked at the blue line of his comrades. They were all staring at him in astonishment. Turning again toward the front, he saw that the enemy soldiers had disappeared. Then he suddenly understood and could only say, "Oh."

The lieutenant was crowing. He called out to the youth, "By heavens, I wish I had 10,000 wildcats like you. Then I could tear the stomach out of this war in less than a week!" The lieutenant puffed out his chest as he said it.

Some of the men were staring at the youth in awe. He had gone on loading and firing and cursing without a stop. Now they looked upon him as a war devil.

Wilson came staggering up to him. "Are

you all right, Fleming? There's nothing the matter with you, Henry—is there?"

"No," said the youth with difficulty. His throat felt sore and tight. Only now did he think about what he had done. It seemed that he had fought against tremendous odds. And he had come out of the struggle a hero.

One of the men had been badly wounded during the fighting. Now he was thrashing about in the grass, twisting his shaking body into strange positions. He started screaming loudly, crying for water.

"Who is it? Who is it?"

"It's Jimmie Rogers. Jimmie Rogers."

Wilson thought he knew where a stream was. He got permission to go for some water. Immediately canteens were showered on him. "Fill mine, will you?" "Bring me some." "Me, too." When Wilson finally left, carrying about a dozen canteens, Henry went along with him.

They made a quick search for the stream but could not find it. "No water here," said the youth. They turned and began to go back.

The two friends carefully made their way through the woods. As they approached a clearing, the general in command of their division rode up with his staff. Just then, another officer galloped into the clearing. He rode up to the general and stopped.

The two unnoticed foot soldiers ducked behind a tree. Henry whispered to his friend, "Let's see if we can hear what they say."

The general looked at the other officer and spoke coolly. "The enemy is forming over there for another charge. It'll be directed against Whiterside. I fear they'll break through unless we stop them. That means we have to charge the enemy *now*. What troops can you spare?"

The officer thought a moment. "Well," he said, "I had to order in the 12th to help the 76th, and I haven't really got any men to spare. But there's the 304th. They fight like a lot of mule drivers. I guess I can spare them the best of any."

Henry and Wilson looked at each other in astonishment. The general spoke sharply. "Get them ready. I'll send word when to start them. It'll be about five minutes."

The officer saluted, wheeled around on

his horse, and started off. As he rode away, the general called out to him, "You should understand—I don't believe many of your mule drivers will get back."

With pale, frightened faces, Henry and Wilson hurried back to the line.

"We're going to charge!" cried Wilson.

"Charge?" said the lieutenant. "*Charge?* Well, by God. Now, we'll see some real fighting!" A boastful smile lit up his face.

The news quickly spread throughout the regiment. A moment later, the officers began to bustle among the men. The youth gave a quick glance at his friend. Wilson looked back at Henry. They were the only ones who knew what the officers had said. *"Mule drivers . . . don't believe many will get back."* A shaggy man near them softly whispered, "We're going to get swallowed."

| 10 |

A Desperate Charge

Henry saw an officer, who looked like a boy on horseback, come galloping toward them. He was waving his hat and shouting orders. Suddenly Henry felt a straining and heaving among the men. The line fell slowly forward like a toppling wall. The youth was pushed and jostled for a moment. Then he lunged ahead and began to run.

As he ran, Henry fixed his eye upon a distant clump of trees. He had decided that the enemy would be met there. He ran toward it as toward a goal.

As the regiment swung from its position into a clearing, the woods seemed to awake. Yellow flames leaped up from many directions. The line of soldiers moved straight ahead for a moment. Then the right wing sprang forward, and then the left.

The youth ran in advance of the others. His eyes kept fixed on the clump of trees. The wild yells of the Rebels could be heard from behind those trees. Little flames of rifle fire leaped from the leaves. The song of bullets was in the air.

Henry felt that he saw *everything*. Each blade of green grass was bold and clear. Every brown or gray tree trunk showed the roughness of its surface.

Still the regiment pressed forward. The men ran in a frenzy, cheering and yelling. Many were hit and fell in terrible agony. A trail of bodies was being left behind.

Finally the men began to lose energy. The leaders began to slacken their speed. The youth had a vague belief that he had run for miles. He thought, in a way, that he was now in some new and unknown land.

Then the men began to notice that their comrades were dropping with moans and shrieks. The regiment stopped its advance. Now the men seemed dazed and stupid. It was a strange pause, and a strange silence.

The sputter of gunfire from the woods became a steady roar. Above this rose the voice of the lieutenant. "Come on, you fools! You can't stay here! You must go on!" His young face was black with rage.

The men stared blankly at the lieutenant. Suddenly, Wilson sprang to life. He lunged forward and dropped to his knees. He fired an angry shot at the enemy. This awakened the men. They, too, began to fire as they slowly moved forward through the trees. Henry thought they moved like a cart stuck in mud, with many jolts and jerks. They halted once again when they came to an open field.

Again the lieutenant began to yell and swear at the men. He grabbed Henry by the arm. "Come on, you lunkhead!" he roared. "We'll all get killed if we stay here. We've only got to go across that field. And then—" The rest of his idea disappeared in a blue haze of curses.

"Cross *there*?" said Henry.

"Certainly. Just cross the field. We can't stay here!" screamed the lieutenant. He started to drag the youth along.

Feeling a sudden anger at the lieutenant, Henry shook him off. "Come on yourself, then," he yelled. They both ran down the front line of the regiment. Wilson ran after them. They stopped in front of the flag. "Come on! Come on!" they yelled. The flag swept toward them. Once again the regiment surged forward.

The scurrying soldiers made their way across the field. Like a madman, the youth ran to reach the woods before a bullet could reach him. As he ran, he ducked his head and nearly closed his eyes. To him, the scene was a wild blur.

Yet within him, as he hurled himself forward, was born a love for this flag that was near him. It was like a woman, red and white, hating and loving, that somehow called him with the voice of his hopes. Somehow he felt that no harm could come to it—and that the flag could be a saver of lives.

Then Henry suddenly became aware that the color sergeant had been hit and was going down. He made a spring for the flagpole and grabbed it. At the same instant, Wilson

grabbed it from the other side. Both of them jerked at the flagpole. But the color sergeant's dead fingers held the flag fast. Finally they pulled the flag away from the dead man. Now Henry and Wilson struggled with it until Henry finally pushed his friend away.

When they looked around, they saw that much of the regiment was in retreat again. The men were headed back to the woods, and the officers were screaming at them. "Where do you think you're going?" howled the lieutenant. "Shoot into 'em! Shoot *into* 'em!"

yelled a red-bearded officer. But the regiment fell back to the trees.

Most of the men seemed stunned—as if they had been betrayed. They glared at the officers, especially at the red-bearded one.

The youth began to feel shame and rage himself. He had thought of a fine revenge on the officer who had called him and his fellows "mule drivers." But now it seemed as if that officer was right after all. To him, the retreat of the mule drivers was a march of shame.

Now Henry ran up and down the regiment, holding the flag high. He added his own loud curses to those of the lieutenant. He tried to drag some of the men on. But it was no use. The regiment was like a machine run down.

Then suddenly a new wave of enemy soldiers sprang from the trees. They were yelling and running toward the regiment. Henry's comrades seemed close to panic.

Wilson ran up to Henry. "Well, Henry, I guess this is goodbye," he said.

"Oh, shut up, you damned fool!" cried Henry. He would not look at Wilson.

Now the officers were trying to beat the men into a proper circle to face the enemy. As well as they could, the men fell to the ground and took cover. The lieutenant cried out, "Here they come! Right onto us, by God!" The rest of his words were lost in a roar of thunder from the men's rifles.

As the smoke slowly lifted, Henry looked at the enemy soldiers. They were so near that he could see the features of their faces.

For a few moments the two bodies of troops traded blows like a pair of boxers. The fast, angry firing went back and forth. Soon there was so much smoke in the air that it was hard to see. Gloomily, Henry seated himself on the ground with the flag between his knees.

After a while the blows of the enemy began to grow weaker. Fewer bullets ripped through the air. Finally, the men could see only dark, floating smoke. Exhausted, they lay still and gazed ahead. As the smoke began to coil away, they saw a ground empty of fighters. It was like a bare stage in a theater—except for the few Rebel corpses that lay twisted into fantastic shapes.

At this sight, many of the men in blue sprang up in a dance of wild joy. Their burning eyes shone, and a cheer broke from their dry lips. They looked around with pride, having gained new trust in the grim weapons in their hands. They felt like men.

| 11 |

Battling On

When no more firing threatened them, the soldiers felt free. At first they drew a long breath of relief. Then they began to show strange emotions. Some of them seemed jumpy and nervous. Others who had fought bravely now could not hide their fear. Weak and shaking, they threw themselves down in the shade of some trees to rest.

Many of them gazed at the ground over which they had charged. Like the others, the youth was struck with amazement. He saw that the distances were very small, even ridiculous. The woods, where so much had taken place, seemed incredibly near. Now that he thought about it, the length of the battle seemed to have been short as well. He wondered at the great number of emotions and events that had been crowded into such little spaces.

Henry looked at his comrades stretched out on the ground. Many were choking with dust, red from perspiration, misty-eyed. Some were gulping at their canteens. Others polished their swollen faces with their coat sleeves and bunches of grass.

Yet the youth felt joy in thinking about his performance during the charge. He was very satisfied.

As the regiment rested, an officer came galloping along the line. It was the general who had called the men "mule drivers." He stopped in front of the colonel.

"What an awful mess you made of this!" he yelled. "Good Lord, man, you stopped about 100 feet short of a very pretty success. But as it is—what a lot of mud diggers you've got, anyway!"

The men, listening, now looked at the colonel. They had an interest in this affair.

The colonel shrugged his shoulders. "Oh, well, General, we went as far as we could," he answered calmly.

"As far as you could? *Did* you, by God?"

snorted the other. "Well, that wasn't very far, was it?" the general added coldly. Then, wheeling his horse, he rode stiffly away.

The lieutenant spoke up to the colonel. "Don't listen to him, sir. Any man who says the boys didn't put up a good fight is a darned fool," he said firmly.

"Lieutenant," began the colonel, "this is my own affair, and I'll trouble you—"

"All right, colonel," said the lieutenant.

News of the officer's remarks passed along the line. It made the men angry. Wilson said, "He must think we went out there and played marbles! I never did see such a man!"

"Oh, well," said Henry, "he probably didn't see much of it at all. He only got mad because we didn't do what he wanted done. It's just our bad luck, that's what."

"I should say so," replied Wilson.

Just then several men came rushing up to Henry and his friend. "Fleming, you should have heard!" cried one, eagerly.

"Heard what?" said the youth.

"Well, we heard the colonel and the lieutenant talking. The colonel wanted to know who carried the flag. When the lieutenant said 'Fleming,' the colonel said, 'He's a good man. He kept the flag way in the front.' 'You bet,' said the lieutenant. 'He and a fellow named Wilson were at the head of the charge.' 'Well, well,' said the colonel, 'they deserve to be major generals.' "

Henry and Wilson gave each other a secret glance of joy and congratulations. Their hearts swelled with grateful affection for the colonel and their loyal lieutenant.

Later, when the woods began to pour forth enemy troops, Henry was full of self-confidence. He looked out calmly at the line of troops forming a blue curve along the side of a hill. He watched the attack begin and smiled when he saw men dodge the shells that were thrown over them.

Henry still held the flag. But he seemed to have forgotten that the flag gave him a role to play. For the moment he was too busy watching the others. The crash and swing of the great drama made him lean forward. He was not even aware of his breathing. Still the flag hung silently over him.

Then a line of Rebel soldiers came within dangerous range. They could be seen plainly—tall, gaunt men with excited faces. They were running with long strides toward a wandering fence.

At the sight of this danger, Henry's comrades quickly raised their rifles and began to fire. No order had been given. Without waiting for a word of command, the men had immediately sent forth a great flock of bullets.

But the enemy soldiers had been quick to gain the protection of the fence. They slid down behind it. From there, they began to slice up the men in blue.

Henry's regiment began to take new losses. Grunting bundles of blue began to drop. The sergeant of the youth's company was shot through the cheek. His jaw hung down, a mass of blood and teeth showing in the wide opening of his mouth. The man tried to cry out, as if he thought that one great shriek would make him well. Then he stumbled off to the rear of the line.

Others fell down about the feet of their companions. Some of the wounded crawled away. But many could only lie still, their bodies twisted into unnatural shapes.

The youth saw the lieutenant holding a position in the rear. He continued to curse. But it was now with the air of a man who was using his last box of oaths. The lieutenant's strong voice was rapidly growing weak.

| 12 |

Victory at Last

"We must go forward!" the colonel shouted from behind the line. Other officers were following close behind him. "We must charge 'em!" they shouted.

Henry saw that his regiment must move ahead. It would be death to stay in their present place. Their best hope was to push the enemy away from the fence.

The men of the regiment seemed to agree. At the shouted words of command, the soldiers sprang forward in eager leaps.

The youth kept the bright flag to the front. Waving his free arm in big circles, he shrieked mad calls, urging the men on. The men in blue seemed to be in a state of frenzy, shouting and cheering. This made Henry run even faster. He felt capable of great sacrifices, a tremendous death. Nothing could stop him from reaching the fence.

As the regiment moved ahead, Henry could see that many of the men in gray were retreating. Only a few of them turned to fire at the advancing blue wave. One part of the Rebel line, however, was held by a grim and stubborn group. These men were settled firmly behind posts and rails. With their flag waving over them, their rifles shot out fiercely.

The youth had fixed his gaze upon the Rebel flag. Its possession would be high pride. Plunging like a mad horse, he went at it. He would not let it escape him.

The men in blue came to a sudden halt at close range. They roared a swift volley. The stubborn group of Rebels was split and broken by the fire. But still they fought. Then the men in blue yelled again and rushed in upon them.

Henry saw five men down on the ground, writhing in pain. The man carrying the Rebel flag had been hit and was having trouble standing on his feet. The look of death was upon his face—but so were the dark and hard lines of desperate purpose. He fought a determined fight.

Wilson leaped over the fence and sprang at the Rebel flag. Pulling it toward him, he wrenched it free with a mad cry. The flag bearer, gasping, lurched over and fell at last. His dead face was turned to the ground.

Henry's regiment broke out into wild cheers. Those who still had hats or caps threw them high into the air.

After the men had celebrated enough, they settled down behind the fence. The youth nestled in some long grass to rest. He leaned his flag against the fence. Wilson came to him there. He was holding his treasure—the Rebel flag. Side by side, the two friends sat and congratulated each other.

The roar of gunfire slowly died away. Only now and then could the boom of artillery be heard in the distance.

The youth arose. "Well, what now, I wonder?" he said. He shaded his eyes with his grimy hand and gazed over the field.

His friend also stood up and said, "I bet we're going to go back over the river."

They waited, watching. Soon the regiment got orders to retrace its way. Henry and Wilson joined the other marching men until their regiment reached the other regiments of the brigade. Now the soldiers marched in a long column through the woods until they finally reached the road.

At this point the division curved away from the field and went off toward the river. Henry looked over his shoulder. Then he said to his friend, "Well, it's all over."

Wilson gazed backward. "By God, it is."

Pictures of the last two days flashed through Henry's mind. He had seen the red of blood and the black of passion, and he had escaped. He remembered his brave deeds and thought about the praise he'd received. He was proud of himself.

But then he reminded himself of his failures. Why had he fled from that first battle? He knew he was not a coward. He must have run because he didn't know any better. Yet he still felt ashamed.

He felt even greater shame when he thought of the tattered soldier. That man, gored by bullets and faint for blood, had worried over Henry's imagined wound. Yet Henry had deserted him in the field. How could he ever forgive himself?

Finally he calmed down. He knew that he couldn't change what had already happened. Perhaps he could learn from it. He had done some good things and some bad things. There was good reason to feel pride as well as guilt. He was but a man, after all.

Now it began to rain. The column of weary soldiers marched through a sea of liquid brown mud. Yet the youth smiled, for he was alive and awake—the nightmare of battle was in the past.

Over the river a golden ray of sun came through the dark rain clouds.

Activities
The Red Badge of Courage

BOOK SEQUENCE

First complete the sentences with words from the box. Then number the events to show which happened first, second, and so on.

battlefield	tattered	Conklin	Wilson	Henry
man	overhear	blankets	guilty	admits
captures	regiment	loading	soldier	

_____ 1. Henry leaves the _____ soldier to wander about helplessly.

_____ 2. Conklin _____ he might run if the other men do.

_____ 3. The lieutenant calls _____ a "war devil."

_____ 4. _____ argues loudly about the rumor the tall soldier heard.

_____ 5. Finding that his friend _____ is badly wounded, Henry tries to help.

_____ 6. For the first time, Henry's _____ is ordered to move out.

_____ 7. Frightened, Henry runs from the _____ and into the woods.

_____ 8. Wilson and Henry _____ some officers talking.

_____ 9. Henry can't remember _____ his rifle.

_____ 10. A fleeing _____ hits Henry with his rifle.

_____ 11. Henry _____ the Rebel flag.

_____ 12. Henry decides that, after all, he is but a _____.

_____ 13. Wilson give Henry his own _____.

_____ 14. Henry feels _____ about leaving the tattered man behind.

81

FACTS ABOUT CHARACTERS

Think about the characters you met in Chapter 1 and answer below.

A. Circle three words that describe each character.

1. **Henry Fleming**

   imaginative   daring   wealthy   thoughtful

   amusing   confident   nervous   noisy

2. **Henry's mother**

   conceited   loving   confused   triumphant

   concerned   furious   ambitious   helpful

3. **Wilson**

   heroic   wild   enthusiastic   embarrassed

   confident   timid   loud   humble

4. **Jim Conklin**

   eager   talkative   unsure   mysterious

   violent   excited   unfriendly   disobedient

B. Who said what? Write a character's name from the box next to each line of dialogue.

Henry Fleming   Henry's mother   Wilson   Jim Conklin

1. _____: "Don't think you can lick the whole Rebel army by yourself!"

2. _____: "Think any of the boys will run?"

3. _____: "Pretty soon you'll find out I was right."

4. _____: "The man that bets on my running will lose his money."

INFERENCE

Reread Chapter 7 and answer below.

A. Circle a letter to show the *implied* (suggested but not stated) meaning of each sentence.

1. Walking slowly toward the campfire,
   Henry could barely stand on his feet.

   a. The ground was too hot to touch.

   b. Henry was very, very tired.

   c. Henry's feet were bare and cold.

2. "Hold on a minute!" Henry cried.
   "What are you going to sleep in?"

   a. Wilson had given Henry his blankets.

   b. Wilson had given Henry his pajamas.

   c. Wilson didn't need to sleep.

3. Henry's head felt as big as a melon.

   a. His head had swollen to twice its size.

   b. His head now weighed thirty pounds.

   c. His head felt puffed up and sore.

4. Wilson said, "I guess I was a pretty
   big fool in those days."

   a. Wilson had graduated from high school.

   b. Wilson had learned not to brag and boast.

   c. Wilson now knew more than the generals.

B. Suppose Wilson had not believed Henry's story.
Do you think he would have made fun of Henry?
If you were Wilson, what would you have done? Why?
Answer in complete sentences.

If I were Wilson _____

_____

_____

_____

Because _____

_____

_____

_____

COMPREHENSION CHECK

Reread Chapter 10 and answer below.

A. Circle a letter to show the correct ending for each
sentence from the story.

1. **Henry ran toward a distant clump of trees**
   a. as toward a goal.
   b. to find a hiding place.

2. **The regiment pressed forward,**
   a. the men running in a frenzy.
   b. the men pausing in a silence.

3. **The youth had a vague belief that he**
   a. had been badly wounded.
   b. had run for miles.

4. **The voice of the lieutenant rose above**
   a. the roar of gunfire.
   b. the brown and gray tree trunks.

B. Write the word from the box that best completes each sentence.

| swear | unknown | flag | fingers | dropped |

1. In a way, Henry felt he was now in some new and _____ land.

2. Springing to life, Wilson lunged forward and _____ to his knees.

3. The lieutenant began to yell and _____ at the men.

4. Henry felt that the _____ could be a saver of lives.

5. The color sergeant's dead _____ held fast to the flagpole.

NOTING DETAILS
Reread Chapter 12 and answer below.

A. Write **T** if the statement is *true* or **F** if the statement is *false*.

1. ___ At the shouted words of command, the soldiers retreated in great leaps.

2. ___ Henry shrieked mad calls, urging the men on.

3. ___ The men in gray seemed to be in a state of frenzy, shouting and cheering.

4. ___ One part of the Yankee line was held by a grim and stubborn group.

5. ___ The look of death was on the face of the Rebel flag bearer.

B. Write one or more words to answer each question.

1. What made Henry run faster and feel "capable of great sacrifices, a tremendous death"?

   _____

   _____

   _____

2. Soldiers on which side were the part of the "advancing blue wave"?

   _____

   _____

   _____

3. What possession would be "high pride" for Henry?

   _____

   _____

   _____

FINAL EXAM

Circle a letter to answer the question or correctly complete each statement.

1. Henry's mother told him
   a. to milk the cow.
   b. not to enlist
   c. to shirk his duty.
   d. not to hurt anyone.

2. Two of Henry's comrades in the regiment were
   a. the corporal and the general.
   b. Jimmie Rogers and Whitherside.
   c. the tall soldier and the loud soldier.
   d. the youth and the mule drivers.

3. After months of boring drills in the camp, Henry
   a. wished he was back on the farm.
   b. was eager to fight.
   c. was glad he enlisted.
   d. bet that Wilson would run away.

4. Henry refused to admit his fear because he
   a. wanted to obey his mother.
   b. thought the other men would laugh at him.
   c. liked all the excitement.
   d. thought the generals were idiots.

5. When did Henry think he had passed "the supreme test?"
   a. when the regiment moved out
   b. when he met the tattered soldier
   c. after the first battle
   d. after grabbing the Union flag

6. After running into the woods, Henry felt
   a. as free as a bird.
   b. angry at Jim Conklin.
   c. pity for other men.
   d. pity for himself.

7. What was the "red badge of courage" Henry envied?
   a. the red Rebel flag
   b. a battle wound
   c. a red velvet medal
   d. red battle ribbons

Answers to Activities
The Red Badge of Courage

BOOK SEQUENCE
1. 7/tattered   2. 2/admits   3. 10/Henry   4. 1/Wilson
5. 6/Conklin   6. 3/regiment   7. 5/battlefield
8. 11/overhear   9. 4/loading   10. 8/soldier
11. 12/captures   12. 14/man   13. 9/blankets
14. 13/guilty

FACTS ABOUT CHARACTERS
A. 1. imaginative, thoughtful, nervous
   2. loving, concerned, helpful
   3. enthusiastic, confident, loud
   4. eager, talkative, excited
B. 1. Henry's mother   2. Henry
   3. Jim Conklin   4. Wilson

INFERENCE
A. 1. b   2. a   3. c   4. b
B. Answers will vary.

COMPREHENSION CHECK
A. 1. a   2. a   3. b   4. a
B. 1. unknown   2. dropped   3. swear   4. flag   5. fingers

NOTING DETAILS
A. 1. F   2. T   3. F   4. F   5. T
B. 1. They were in a frenzy, shouting and cheering.
   2. Union or Yankee soldiers.
   3. the Rebel flag

FINAL EXAM
1. b   2. c   3. a   4. b   5. c   6. d   7. b